Best Friends

I wish, I wish
With all *my* heart
To fly with dragons
In a land apart.

By Margaret Snyder
Based on the characters by Ron Rodecker
Illustrated by Bob Berry

A Random House PICTUREBACK® Book

Random House 🏠 New York

Library of Congress Cataloging-in-Publication Data
Snyder, Margaret.
Best friends / by Margaret Snyder ; based on the characters by Ron Rodecker ; illustrated by Bob Berry.
p. cm. — (A Random House pictureback book)
SUMMARY: Best friends Cassie and Emmy venture into the Dandelion Forest to gather sunshine lemonade.
ISBN 0-375-81389-6 [1. Best friends—Fiction. 2. Friendship—Fiction. 3. Lemonade—Fiction.] I. Rodecker, Ron. II. Berry, Bob, ill.
III. Title. IV. Random House pictureback. PZ7.S685177 Be 2001 [E]—dc21 00-068324

www.randomhouse.com/kids/sesame
Visit Dragon Tales on the Web at www.dragontales.com
Printed in the United States of America   October 2001   10 9 8 7 6 5 4 3 2 1

"What a perfect day for a tea party," said Cassie to her best friend. Cassie giggled as she cut an imaginary piece of cake and served it to Emmy.

"I'm happy we thought of doing this," Emmy said. She tipped her teacup to look inside. "But all this pretending is making me thirsty for real."

Cassie thought for a moment, and then a big smile spread over her face. "You know what would be great for a tea party? Some sunshine lemonade!"

"What's that?" asked Emmy. "It sounds yummy!"

"It's made from rain that falls when the sun is out," Cassie
told her. "It collects in the tiny flowers that grow deep in the
Dandelion Forest."

Emmy jumped up. "That sounds great," she said. "Let's go!"

"Maybe it's not such a good idea after all," Cassie said, hesitating. "Those dandelions can get pretty grumpy! I bet they won't like us being in their forest."

"Well, how good *is* sunshine lemonade?" Emmy asked.

"As good as dragonberry muffins!" Cassie said with a grin. "Let's go!"

Emmy grabbed the pitcher and climbed onto Cassie's back. In a minute, the two friends were zooming high over Dragon Land.

Soon they arrived at the forest. The sound of the dandelions' snores reached the girls as they landed close by.

"Good! The dandelions are sleeping!" Cassie whispered. "We have to be really, *really* quiet now. If we wake them up, they'll start roaring something awful."

As they tiptoed through the forest, Emmy started to giggle.

"Shh," Cassie whispered to Emmy. But then she began to giggle, too.

"I can't help it," Emmy said, trying to muffle her snickers and snorts. "It's hard to be quiet when you've got the giggles!"

Soon, Emmy and Cassie were right in the middle of the snoozing dandelions. On the ground were hundreds of tiny, cup-shaped flowers tucked between the dandelion stalks.

"They look like little teacups!" Emmy whispered.

Cassie nodded. "See the sunshine lemonade inside?" she said quietly. "We'll have to empty a lot of flowers to fill our pitcher."

"I can't wait to have a sip!" Emmy whispered. Caught up in the excitement, she rushed toward one of the flowers. Just then, something went *crunch* beneath Emmy's feet.

"Watch out!" Cassie cried out softly, pointing to the ground. "There are dandelion seeds everywhere."

Cassie was right. And more seeds popped as Emmy took another careful step.

Crunch. Crunch. Crunch.

"Oops!" Emmy whispered. She quickly jumped onto a ball of dandelion fluff.

"Cassie, I have an idea! I think this fluff can help us get the lemonade," Emmy whispered, pointing to her feet.

Cassie knew at once what her best friend was thinking. The fluff would muffle their footsteps! Emmy grabbed some dandelion fluff and soon they were hard at work shaping it into soft, puffy shoes.

When they were finished, Cassie and Emmy looked as if they were wearing big, fuzzy bedroom slippers. "These are perfect," Cassie whispered. "Now we won't make any noise."

"Definitely!" Emmy whispered back.

The two girls shuffled toward the little flowers. Cassie began emptying the blossoms one by one into Emmy's pitcher. The scent of lemons filled the air.

Soon the pitcher was filled to the brim with sunshine lemonade. Cassie signaled to Emmy that it was time to go. But Emmy held up her finger, motioning to Cassie to wait. The lemony nectar smelled so delicious. Emmy just *had* to try some now.

Using a flower as a cup, Emmy tipped the lemony nectar into her mouth. Yum! It was the best she had ever tasted!

"This is *sooooo* good!" Emmy blurted out.

The dandelions blinked their sleepy lids in surprise, and Cassie looked around in alarm. "Oh, no!" she cried.

"**GRRRRR!**" the dandelions growled. "**ARRRRR! ROAR!**"

"Let's get out of here!" both girls shouted at the same time. In seconds, they were flying high in the air, leaving the roaring dandelions far below.

"Whew! That was a close call," said Cassie as she and Emmy landed safely back at their tea table. Then she burst into giggles, waggling her fluffy, puffy slippers in delight over their adventure.

"That was a blast!" Emmy said as she happily poured sunshine lemonade into the teacups.

"Now it's a real party," Cassie said. She raised her cup of lemonade. "To my very best friend," she said, "and our best adventure yet!"

"There's just one thing, though," Emmy said as she tapped her teacup against Cassie's. "This adventure has made me hungry. Isn't there somewhere we can get something to eat?"